NIGHT
at the
FAIR

pictures and words by
Donald Crews

Greenwillow Books · New York

*For family,
friends, and
fans — have fun
at the fair.*

For Jack

*Watercolors and
gouache paints
were used for
the full-color art.
The text type is
Akzidenz Grotesk.*

*Greenwillow Books,
a division of William
Morrow & Company, Inc.,
10 East 53rd Street,
New York, NY 10022.
Manufactured in China.
First Edition
12 13 SCP 20 19 18 17 16*

*Library of Congress
Cataloging-in-Publication Data*

*Crews, Donald.
Night at the fair / by Donald Crews.
p.   cm.
Summary: Nighttime is a wonderful
time to enjoy the lights, the games,
and the rides at the fair.
ISBN 0-688-11483-0 (trade)
ISBN 0-688-11484-9 (lib. bdg.)
[1. Fairs—Fiction.   2. Night—Fiction.]
I. Title.   PZ7.C8683Nf   1997
[E]—dc21   96-48780   CIP   AC*

Nighttime is a great time to be at the fair. Black skies, bright lights sparkling.

So many
games
to play.

So many
prizes.

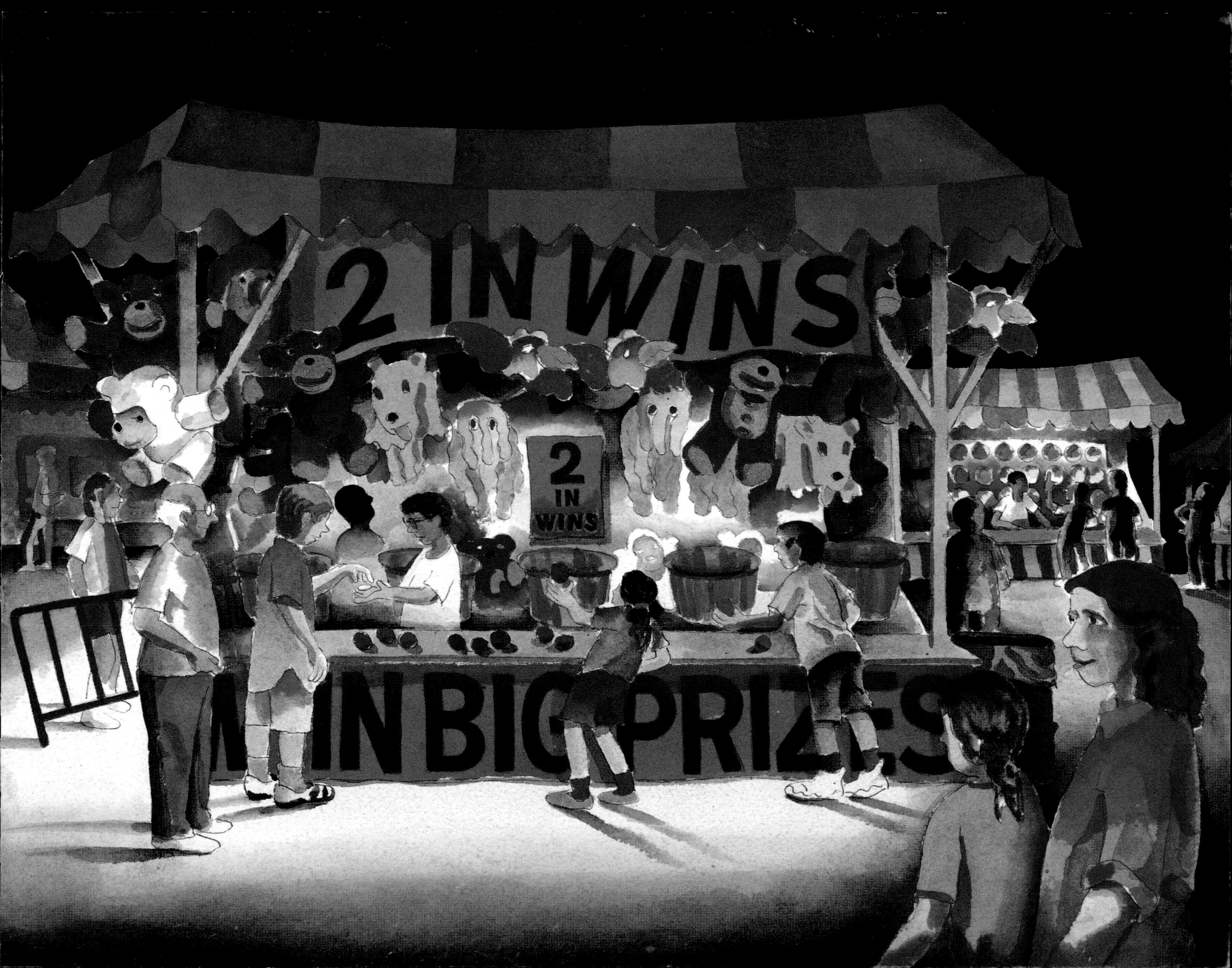

And now,
on to the
RIDES!

The best,
the best
ride of all,
is the GIANT
FERRIS
WHEEL!

We get
on at the
bottom, and
when we get to
the top, we'll see
the whole fair.
EVERYTHING!
We'll see where
we've been and
where we can
still go.

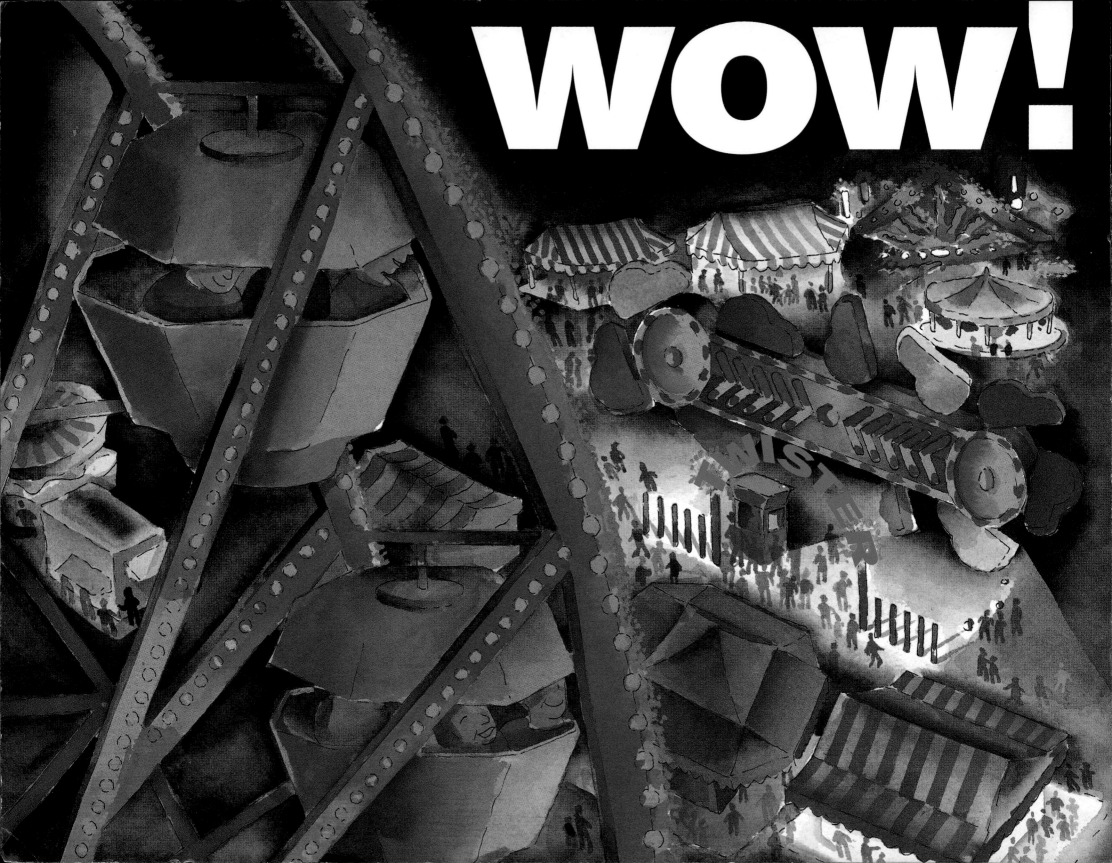